Did You Hear?

A Story
About
Gossip

by Frank J. Sileo, PhD
illustrated by Jennifer Zivoin

MAGINATION PRESS • WASHINGTON, DC

American Psychological Association

To my sister Theresa and my brother Sal: Thanks for being my awesome confidantes—*FJS*

For Olivia and Elyse, my two favorite chatterboxes—*JZ*

Published by
MAGINATION PRESS®
An Educational Publishing Foundation Book
American Psychological Association
750 First Street NE
Washington, DC 20002

Magination Press is a registered trademark of the American Psychological Association.
For more information about our books, including a complete catalog, please write to us,
call 1-800-374-2721, or visit our website at www.apa.org/pubs/magination.

Book design by Susan K. White
Printed by Worzalla, Stevens Point, WI

Library of Congress Cataloging-in-Publication Data
Names: Sileo, Frank J., 1967- author. | Zivoin, Jennifer, illustrator.
Title: Did you hear? : a story about gossip / by Frank J. Sileo, PhD ; illustrated by Jennifer Zivoin.
Description: Washington, DC : Magination Press, [2017] | "American Psychological Association."
Summary: "Gives examples of serious and silly gossip, leading to what hurtful gossip feels like,
how it is like bullying, and what to do to stop it"— Provided by publisher.
Identifiers: LCCN 2016050574 | ISBN 9781433827204 (hardcover) | ISBN 1433827204 (hardcover)
Subjects: | CYAC: Stories in rhyme. | Gossip—Fiction. | Conduct of life—Fiction.
Classification: LCC PZ8.3.S58254 Di 2017 | DDC [E]—dc23 LC record available at
https://lccn.loc.gov/2016050574

Manufactured in the United States of America
10 9 8 7 6 5 4 3 2

Did you hear Eric picks his nose?
Did you hear Alexa has eleven toes?

Did you hear Luke held Tina's hand in the hall?

This **gossip** might be false or might be true.
It can happen to or be spread by you.

Did you hear Sam didn't make the team and cried?

Did you hear Carla pushed Dave off the slide?

Did you hear Claire
has a crush on Tim?

Did you hear Michael
has a crush on Jim?

Gossip can spread online, by text, or from ear to ear.
You might be interested in what you read or hear.

Gossip can be just like the game of telephone,
when the story changes and gets overblown.

Sometimes these stories end up amusing!
But knowing what's true can be confusing.

It doesn't matter if the story is true.
Gossip can make others angry or blue.

Did you hear Adam's breath smells like Brussels sprouts?

Sometimes a gossiper means no harm
but the things they say could cause alarm.

Did you hear Noah's dog went to the vet?
Did you hear Sylvia's dad owns a jet?

A gossiper might be seen as a bully
even if they don't mean it hurtfully.

Did you hear Max lost his brand new backpack?

What are you to do when
unkind gossip comes your way?
Don't repeat or listen to
what the gossip has to say.

Did you hear Miss Parker told Emily she couldn't sing?

Did you hear Diego got sent to the principal for burping?

Did you hear Aimee passed gas in class?
Did you hear Billy broke the window glass?

If the gossip you hear is about a friend or you,
tell them gossiping is an unkind thing to do.

Talk to an adult, at home or at school.
They understand gossiping just isn't cool.

Be careful with private things and what you say.
Do all you can to keep mean gossip away.

Treat others the way you would like to be treated.
How you would feel if your private things were repeated?

Next time you hear gossip, take a stand.
Help one another before it gets out of hand.

So if someone says, "Did you hear...this or that,"
tell them you're not interested in gossip
and refuse to chat.

Note to Parents and Caregivers

We have all probably found ourselves in the position where we heard an interesting piece of gossip from another person. As social beings, we are often inherently fascinated by gossip and want to share information with others. We are captivated and entertained by the shocking headlines on magazines, newspapers, gossip websites, and talk shows.

What Is Gossip?

It seems everyone gossips or at least listens to gossip. Gossip is likely going around your community, school, club, work, etc. It is often idle talk about others, but can also be about subjects that are shocking or personal, including relationships or other private matters that people would prefer to keep to themselves. Gossip typically occurs behind someone's back and can be true or false.

Gossip is not always harmful. It can be viewed as a way of sharing information and staying connected with other people's lives. For example, asking "how is Katie doing after her bicycle accident?" might be considered gossip, but there is no malicious intent to talk about a person in a negative way. Gossip becomes a problem when it is used to harm others, whether intentionally or not. When we tell stories that may not be true, reveal information that is meant to be kept private, or say hurtful things about others, we are spreading gossip in a harmful way. There is also always the danger that gossip that starts small and seems innocent can grow into something problematic or harmful.

Why Do Children Gossip?

As mentioned, gossiping is often a natural and typical human behavior; many times, it is done without much thought. However, it is also often used to achieve some type of goal. Children may engage in gossiping...

To Feel Better Than Others

When children feel bad about themselves, sometimes they will try to make someone else feel worse so that they feel better. Feelings of jealousy may cause some children to try to bring the other person down by spreading hurtful gossip. Similarly, revenge is also a common motive for hurtful gossip. Children may also use gossip as a way of being perceived as knowing more than others or believe that if they share gossip with others they may gain popularity.

To Get Attention

All children want attention. When a child knows something that others do not or is the first person to hear gossip, it can make the child the center of attention. For the child who may feel inadequate or insecure, gossip may be a way to gain attention, even if it is for a short time. We also know that children will act out to gain attention, and spreading gossip can be a form of acting-out behavior.

To Feel Included

Children want to have a sense of belonging with others, to be part of a group. They may experience peer pressure from others to gossip about someone or something. This puts them in a difficult social position; even if they do not want to gossip, they may feel they have to participate in order to fit in and avoid being excluded. They may also have concerns about becoming a future target if they do not join the gossipers.

For Control

Sometimes children want to be in control or be popular. One avenue of maintaining control or achieving top social status is to reduce the control or popularity of someone else, and spreading hurtful gossip is a common way to do this. We see this all the time in adult political campaigns as well; one candidate will often try to better their status by smearing their opponents.

When Bored

Children will sometimes start spreading gossip simply because they are bored. Gossiping about others may spice things up a bit by eliciting a reaction in others and even causing people to fight.

When children are more productive and active in their lives, they are less likely to gossip.

When Gossiping Becomes Bullying

While a child may not gossip with the overt intention of bullying others, the act of starting or spreading hurtful gossip can be seen as (or simply become) a form of bullying. With today's technology, gossip can spread faster and further than ever before. Writing and distributing harmful gossip online is known as cyber-bullying. Cyber-bullying has been a growing problem in recent years; it is easy for children to hide behind their computer screens or phones and write anonymously hurtful things about others. Parents need to monitor what their children are putting up on social media sites and how they are using technology.

Words can hurt. Malicious gossip has the potential to be just as psychologically harmful as physical bullying. Being a victim of gossip can make a child feel isolated and helpless, leading to lowered self-esteem. In the worst cases, this can even lead to depression and drive children to engage in suicidal thoughts and behaviors.

Be aware of some warning signs that your child is being bullied. They may want to avoid school, friends, and other social activities that were once enjoyed, and may seem uncharacteristically moody and tearful. Physical complaints, like recurrent stomach or head aches, difficulty sleeping (and possibly nightmares when they do sleep), and decreased appetite could be signs of stress from bullying. Declining school performance is also often seen. If your child is exhibiting these symptoms, speak with your child, their school, and, if necessary, a mental health professional.

Preventing Hurtful Gossip

Gossip stops with you! Even adults can feel the urge to gossip or "dish" with friends, co-workers, significant others, and other parents. We live in a reality television culture where we glorify backstabbing and cruel interactions. When this behavior is accepted as normal, we are directly modeling tolerance for cruel actions, including gossip. Children need to learn appropriate treatment of others, no matter whether it's in-person or on social media and other technology.

Set an Example

We need to be aware of what we say and do in front of our children. We also need to be careful of our posts on social media, particularly when children are old enough to see them. When we find our children spreading harmful gossip about others, we need to address it right away.

Teach Empathy

We want to help children to be empathic—to understand the feelings of others. When you talk with your children, ask them, "Would you want people to know private stuff about you?", "How will the person feel if others know their private information?", "Are you being a trustworthy friend?" and "What do you get out of telling private things about others?" When you explore these questions with your child, you can help them to be more sensitive to the feelings of others, which makes it easier to decide the right thing to do.

Don't Be an Audience

When we refuse to listen or be an audience to people gossiping, we send the message that gossip isn't important to us. Some people spread gossip for attention or power, and a disinterested audience takes that motivation away. Teach children to say something like, "I don't like talking about others that way" or to simply walk away and not participate in the conversation. Understand that it may be very tempting to stay and listen, because sometimes gossip can be very interesting, especially if one is bored. But a gossiper can only continue gossiping if people are willing to listen.

Respect Privacy

We want to teach children that if they want their personal things kept private, they should respect the privacy of others. Acknowledge their feelings of temptation to share something interesting that they might hear from others, but emphasize that others' feelings are more important. We should encourage our children to keep their private information private, both in person and (especially) on the Internet and social media platforms. Children need to know that once something is posted online, it is very difficult to delete. Educate children to use good judgment on whom they confide in.

An important caveat to not sharing private information is if they hear an unsafe secret, such as if someone is being hurt. Encourage your child to talk with a trusted grown-up about what the next step should be if they hear about something dangerous or inappropriate, or are unsure about how to help keep a friend or peer safe.

If your child has been the recipient of hurtful gossip or continues to gossip with others, it may be important to consult with a licensed mental health professional to discuss the issue. They may be able to help your child understand their underlying need to start and spread hurtful gossip to others. If your child is the recipient of malicious gossip, a professional can help them cope with what has happened and give them strategies to deal with hurtful words.

About the Author

FRANK J. SILEO, PHD, is a New Jersey licensed psychologist and the founder and executive director of The Center for Psychological Enhancement in Ridgewood, New Jersey. He received his doctorate from Fordham University in New York City. In his practice, Dr. Sileo works with children, adolescents, adults, and families. Since 2010, he has been consistently recognized as one of New Jersey's top kids' doctors. He is the author of six other children's books: *Toilet Paper Flowers: A Story for Children About Crohn's Disease, Hold the Cheese Please: A Story for Children About Lactose Intolerance, Bug Bites and Campfires: A Story for Kids About Homesickness, Sally Sore Loser: A Story about Winning and Losing, Don't Put Yourself Down in Circus Town: A Story About Self-Confidence* and *A World of Pausabilities: An Exercise in Mindfulness.* His books *Sally Sore Loser, Don't Put Yourself Down in Circus Town,* and *A World of Pausabilities* are the Gold Medal recipients of the prestigious Mom's Choice Awards. He has also won Silver Medals from the Moonbeam Children's Book Awards and the Independent Publisher Book Awards. Dr. Sileo speaks across the country and does author visits. Dr. Sileo has been published in psychological journals and is often quoted in newspapers, magazines, podcasts, webcasts, radio, and television. Learn more about Dr. Sileo on his website, drfranksileo.com.

About the Illustrator

Like many of the characters in this book, JENNIFER ZIVOIN was quite a chatterbox as a child! She has always loved stories and art, so becoming an illustrator was a natural career path. She has been trained in media ranging from figure drawing to virtual reality, and earned her Bachelor of Arts degree with highest distinction from the honors division of Indiana University. During her professional career, Jennifer worked as a graphic designer and then as a creative director before finding her artistic niche illustrating children's books. In addition to artwork, she enjoys reading, cooking, and spending time outdoors. Jennifer lives in Indiana with her family.

Jennifer is a member of the Society of Children's Book Writers & Illustrators and is represented by MB Artists.

About Magination Press

MAGINATION PRESS is an imprint of the American Psychological Association, the largest scientific and professional organization representing psychologists in the United States and the largest association of psychologists worldwide.